THE HARVEST BIRDS
los pájaros de la cosecha

Story by/Escrito por BLANCA LÓPEZ DE MARISCAL
Pictures by/Ilustrado por ENRIQUE FLORES

Children's Book Press   •   San Francisco, California

In a little town where everyone knew everyone, there lived a young man called Juan Zanate. He was given this name because he was always accompanied by one or two zanate birds.

Juan used to sit under his favorite tree, dreaming and planning his life. He wanted to have his own land, as his father and grandfather had. But when his father died and the land was divided, there was only enough for his two older brothers. So Juan had to hire himself out to shopkeepers in the town.

En un pueblecito donde toda la gente se conocía, vivía un joven que todos llamaban Juan Zanate. Lo llamaban así porque siempre estaba acompañado de uno o varios zanates.

A Juan le gustaba sentarse bajo un árbol y ponerse ahí a soñar y planear su vida. Él quería tener su propia tierra, como su padre y su abuelo. Pero cuando murió su padre, la pequeña tierra que se repartió sólo alcanzó para los dos hermanos mayores. Por eso Juan se vio obligado a trabajar haciendo muchos oficios en el pueblo.

f only I had my own land, my life would be different," thought Juan. Once, he went to see Don Tobías, the richest man in town, and asked to borrow a little piece of land.

Don Tobías burst out laughing, and his wife laughed with him. "Why should I give you land? You don't know anything about making things grow."

i tan sólo tuviera mi propia tierra, mi vida sería tan diferente", pensaba Juan. Un día fue a ver a don Tobías, el rico del pueblo, y le pidió que le prestara un pequeño pedazo de tierra.

Don Tobías se echó a reír a carcajadas y su esposa se rió con él: —¿Por qué debiera darte tierra? Tú no sabes ni sembrar el campo.

Sad and ashamed, Juan returned to sit under his favorite tree. It was the only place where he felt really happy. In its enormous branches lived a flock of zanate birds who were so used to his presence that they considered him their friend.

There was one bird in particular who cared very much for Juan and wanted him to find his way in life. This bird was always around Juan, resting on his shoulder or on the brim of his hat. Juan named him Grajo.

Juan se retiró triste y molesto a la sombra de su árbol. Era el único lugar en que se encontraba realmente feliz. En las enormes ramas vivía una parvada de zanates que estaban tan acostumbrados a su presencia, que ya lo consideraban un amigo.

Había un zanate en especial que se preocupaba por Juan y quería que éste encontrara su camino en la vida. Estaba siempre muy cerca de Juan, se paraba en su hombro o en el ala de su sombrero. Juan lo llamaba Grajo.

After sitting and thinking for a long time, Juan decided to visit the old man of the town. "Old people know many things because they've lived longer," thought Juan. "Surely he'll give some advice, and maybe he'll even help me."

Después de pensar y pensar por mucho tiempo, Juan decidió ir a platicar con el viejo del pueblo. "Los viejos, porque han vivido más, saben mucho", pensó. "Seguramente él me podrá aconsejar, y puede ser que hasta me dé su ayuda".

J uan greeted the old man, whom everyone called Grandpa Chon, with respect. The old man looked at him for a few moments and asked, "Have you just been sitting under your tree, Juan?"

"Yes," answered Juan, very curious. "But how did you know?"

"When you have lived longer, little Juan, you will see that by watching carefully and observing, you come to know many things," replied Grandpa Chon.

J uan saludó al viejo, al que todos llamaban Tata Chon, con respeto. "Tata" significa abuelo. El viejo se le quedó viendo por unos instantes y luego le preguntó: —¿Juan, vienes de estar sentado bajo tu árbol?

—Sí —contestó Juan, lleno de curiosidad—. Pero ¿cómo lo supo?

—Cuando vivas más, pequeño Juan, te darás cuenta de que observando, observando, uno llega a saber muchas cosas —respondió Tata Chon.

es, but how did you know?" insisted Juan. "My tree is a long way from here."

"Look at your hat, Juan. You can tell that the birds have been flying around above you." Grandpa Chon laughed. But it was not mocking laughter, like that of Don Tobías and his wife. This time it was friendly laughter.

 í, pero cómo lo supo?
—insistió Juan—. Mi árbol está muy lejos de aquí.

—Fíjate en tu sombrero Juan. Bien se nota que los zanates han estado revoloteando encima de ti —Tata Chon echó a reír, sólo que esta vez la risa no era de burla, como la de don Tobías y su esposa, sino que era una risa de amistad.

When Juan realized that Grandpa Chon was in a good mood, he dared to ask him for a piece of land. "Let me prove to you that I can be a good farmer and make things grow," he pleaded.

Grandpa Chon became serious. "I will help you," he said. "I will lend you land. But remember, if you fail, you must work for me for free for as many days as you have used my land."

Al darse cuenta Juan del buen humor del abuelo, se atrevió a pedirle un pedazo de tierra: —Déjeme que le demuestre que yo puedo ser un buen campesino y cultivar la tierra —le imploró Juan.

Tata Chon se puso serio. —Te voy a ayudar —le dijo el viejo—. Te voy a prestar la tierra pero con una condición: si fracasas, me vas a pagar con trabajo el tiempo que ocupes mi terreno.

uan ran into the town, shouting his good news. But instead of being happy for him, people mocked him.

"Better you should straighten up my workshop, because where you plant, not even wildflowers will grow," shouted the carpenter.

"Don't waste your time Juan, come work on this wheel," called the blacksmith.

"Help me with these sacks of flour and stop dreaming," added the baker.

uan corrió de gusto, gritando la noticia. Pero en vez de compartir su alegría, la gente se burló de él.

—¡Mejor ven a arreglar mi taller, porque donde tú siembres ni flores del campo se van a dar! —le gritó el carpintero.

—¡No pierdas el tiempo Juan, y ven a trabajar en esta rueda! —le dijo el herrero.

—¡Ayúdame con estos sacos de harina, y deja ya de soñar! —le ordenó el panadero.

ut Juan decided that nothing anyone said would stop him. "It's time to get to work," he said to himself. He began to prepare his land for planting. It was a very tiny plot of land and didn't offer much promise of a big harvest. Still, Juan kept on working, accompanied by his loyal friends, the zanates.

"My head is also small, but it is big enough to hold many dreams," thought Juan.

uan decidió que lo que pensaran los demás no lo iba a detener. "Llegó el momento de ponerme a trabajar", se dijo. Así empezó a preparar el terreno para cultivarlo. Era muy pequeño y no daba muchas esperanzas de una gran cosecha. Pero Juan siguió trabajando acompañado de sus inseparables amigos, los zanates.

"Mi cabeza también es pequeña y en ella caben muchos sueños", pensó Juan.

Juan needed seeds to plant, but didn't have money to buy them, so he went to the shopkeeper and asked him for some seeds.

"Juan, sweep up the corn, the beans and the squash seeds from my floor and take them to my pigs. Then, if you wish, you can take some seeds for yourself."

Como Juan necesitaba semillas para plantar y no tenía dinero para comprarlas, fue a ver al tendero y le pidió algunas semillas fiadas.

—Juan, barre los granos de maíz, los frijoles y las semillas de calabaza que han caído al suelo y dáselas a mis puercos. Y si te sirven algunas de estas semillas, te las puedes llevar.

uan was happy, because now he had seeds to plant. He didn't scare away the zanates the way the other farmers did. Instead, he gave them some of his leftover seeds to eat so they wouldn't be hungry and steal the seeds he was planting. After all, the zanates were his friends and companions, and he cared for them very much. Grajo was always with him, giving advice in his hoarse voice.

uan estaba feliz pues ya tenía semillas para plantar. No corrió a los zanates como lo hace la mayoría de los campesinos. En vez de eso, decidió apartar algunas de las semillas que sobraron para que los zanates tuvieran qué comer y no se robaran las que estaba plantando en los surcos. Después de todo, los zanates eran sus amigos y sus acompañantes, y Juan se preocupaba mucho por ellos. Grajo, que estaba siempre junto a Juan, le daba consejos con su áspera voz.

ays passed, and the zanates guided Juan as he worked. When the tiny plants began to appear and little shoots of weeds along with them, the zanates told Juan not to throw the weeds away as the other farmers did.

"Plant them on the borders of your land," said the birds.

When the other farmers heard what Juan was doing, they laughed at him. "Imagine keeping weeds in your field!"

asaron los días y los zanates guiaban la labor de Juan. Cuando comenzaron a salir las pequeñas plantas y con ellas los brotes de hierbas silvestres, los zanates le dijeron a Juan que no las arrancara ni las tirara a la basura como lo hacían los otros campesinos.

—Siémbralas en los bordes del terreno —le dijeron los zanates.

Cuando los otros campesinos supieron lo que Juan hacía, se burlaron de él: —¡Qué locura, dejar crecer hierba silvestre en la parcela!

At harvest time, everyone was waiting to make fun of Juan once again. They were sure he would fail. But when Juan arrived in town, everyone was astonished. He brought a magnificent harvest: huge ears of corn, brilliantly-colored squashes, and delicious-looking beans.

Cuando se llegó el tiempo de la cosecha, todos esperaban burlarse de Juan una vez más. Todos estaban seguros que él iba a fracasar. Pero cuando Juan llegó al pueblo todos quedaron maravillados. En su cargamento Juan traía una magnífica cosecha: enormes mazorcas, calabazas de colores brillantes y apetitosos frijoles.

ow did you do it?" they all wanted to know. Juan smiled and answered, "I did it with the help of my friends the zanates, the harvest birds. I learned to listen very carefully, over and over, to the voice of nature!"

"Work with me, Juan!" everyone shouted. "Teach us your secrets!"

"No," answered the old man, "Juan works for no one now, because I am going to give him the land that he harvested."

ómo lo había logrado? —todos querían saber. Juan se sonrió y respondió: —Con la ayuda de mis amigos los zanates, los pájaros de la cosecha; observando, observando he sabido escuchar la voz de la naturaleza.

—¡Trabaja conmigo Juan! —decían todos a voces—. ¡Enséñanos tus secretos!

—No —contestó el viejo—, Juan ya no trabajará para nadie, porque le voy a regalar el terreno que cosechó.

After selling their crop at an excellent price, Juan Zanate and Grandpa Chon returned together to the little plot of land which was now Juan's. The old man asked Juan to tell him his secret.

"The zanates taught me that all plants are like brothers and sisters," replied Juan. "If you separate them, they become sad and won't grow. But if you respect them and leave them together, they will grow happily and be content."

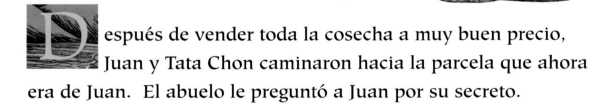

Después de vender toda la cosecha a muy buen precio, Juan y Tata Chon caminaron hacia la parcela que ahora era de Juan. El abuelo le preguntó a Juan por su secreto.

—Los zanates me enseñaron que todas las plantas son como hermanos y hermanas —replicó Juan—. Si uno las aparta, se ponen tristes y no crecen fuertes y sanas. Pero si uno las respeta y las deja juntas, crecen muy felices y contentas.

THE HARVEST BIRDS / LOS PÁJAROS DE LA COSECHA is a folktale from the oral tradition of Oaxaca, Mexico. Like many folktales, it passes on scientific truths as well as moral values. By planting weeds around his land, Juan helps prevent erosion from winds and torrential rains coming down from the mountains. When he plants corn, squash and beans together, they thrive better than they would apart because each brings something the others need. Some folktales refer to corn, squash and beans as "the three sisters" because of this close relationship.

Blanca López de Mariscal is a teacher from Monterrey, Mexico. She researches the literature of ancient Mexico and is especially interested in the oral tradition of her Mexican ancestors. She thinks that people living in urban environments have a lot to learn from those who live in contact with nature.

Enrique Flores lives with his family in the beautiful Mexican village of Huitzo, outside the city of Oaxaca. He creates his paintings and graphics in a lilac-colored studio which he built himself on a hilltop above the house. From his window he can see the zanate birds flying over the fields and nesting in the trees.

Story copyright ©1995 by Blanca López de Mariscal. All rights reserved.
Illustrations copyright ©1995 by Enrique Flores. All rights reserved.
English version of the story copyright ©1995 by Children's Book Press. All rights reserved.
Editors: Harriet Rohmer and David Schecter
Consulting Editor: Francisco X. Alarcón
Design and Production: Nancy Hom   Production Consultant: Pamela Wilson   Photography: Lee Fatherree
Special thanks go to Nancy Mayagoitia, Director of Arte de Oaxaca, for helping to make this book possible.

Distributed to the book trade by Publishers Group West. Quantity discounts available through the publisher for educational and nonprofit use. Children's Book Press is a nonprofit publisher of multicultural and bilingual literature for children, supported in part by grants from the California Arts Council. To receive a free catalog, write: Children's Book Press, 2211 Mission Street, San Francisco, CA 94110. Visit us at www.cbookpress.org.

Library of Congress Cataloging-in-Publication Data
López de Mariscal, Blanca.

The harvest birds = Los pájaros de la cosecha / story by Blanca López de Mariscal; pictures by Enrique Flores.   p.   cm.
Summary: A young man realizes his dream by listening to the voice of nature.
ISBN 0-89239-169-3 (paperback)
[1.Folklore—Mexico. 2.Spanish language materials—Bilingual.]
I. Flores, Enrique, ill. II.Title.   III. Title: Pájaros de la cosecha.
PZ73.L727   1995   94-40016   CIP   AC

Printed in Hong Kong through Marwin Productions

10   9   8   7   6   5   4   3   2   1